HOCKEY MELTDOWN

BY JAKE MADDOX

TEXT BY
CHRIS KREIE

ILLUSTRATIONS BY
SEAN TIFFANY

ake Maddox books are published by Stone Arch Books
A Capstone Imprint
.51 Good Counsel Drive, P.O. Box 669
Mankato, Minnesota 56002
www.capstonepub.com

Library of Congress Cataloging-in-Publication Data
Maddox, Jake.
Hockey meltdown / by Jack Maddox ; text by Chris Kreie ; illustrated by Sean Tiffany.
p. cm. -- (Jake Maddox sports story)
Summary: Although Dylan's wrist is healing from the pre-season injury, can he be part of the team if he is stuck on the bench?
ISBN 978-1-4342-2990-8 (library binding) -- ISBN 978-1-4342-3426-1 (pbk.)
1. Hockey stories. 2. Sports teams--Juvenile fiction. 3. Teamwork (Sports)--Juvenile fiction. [1. Hockey--Fiction. 2. Teamwork (Sports)--Fiction.] I. Kreie, Chris. II. Tiffany, Sean, ill. III. Title.
PZ7.M25643Hk 2012
[Fic]--dc22

2011000347

Art Director: Kay Fraser
Graphic Designer: Russell Griesmer
Production Specialist: Michelle Biedscheid

Photo Credits: Shutterstock/Brian Paulson (cover)

Printed in the United States of America in Stevens Point, Wisconsin.
032011
006111WZF11

TABLE OF CONTENTS

CHAPTER 1
THERE GOES THE SEASON

Dylan Marshall stood on top of the skate ramp at Iron Valley Skate Park. He balanced on his skates and looked down at the pavement six feet below him.

His best friends, Nick Shaw and Tommy Reyes, stood on the sidelines, cheering.

"Come on, Dylan!" Nick yelled. "You can do it, man!"

Dylan wiped the sweat from his forehead.

Then, taking a deep breath, he used his back skate to push off. He shot down the ramp, picking up major speed. He reached the bottom of the ramp and flew across the pavement.

The wheels on his skates rotated rapidly as Dylan hit the next ramp. He kept his knees bent. As he reached the top of the ramp, he straightened his legs and jumped.

Dylan was flying. He kicked both feet to the right and reached down to grab his skates. His body whipped around in a complete circle. Then he released the grip on his skates and landed smoothly on the pavement. He skidded to a perfect stop.

"That was awesome!" Tommy yelled, skating over to Dylan.

"Thanks," said Dylan.

The boys skated over to a picnic table at the edge of the skate park and sat down.

"Can you believe school starts next week?" asked Dylan. He took a long sip from his water bottle.

"Ugh! Did you have to bring that up?" asked Tommy. He groaned.

"But if school starts soon, hockey season is just a few weeks away," Nick pointed out.

"I guess that makes me feel a little better," Tommy muttered.

"We're going to dominate this season," said Nick.

"Do you think we can win the Midwinter Meltdown Tournament?" asked Tommy.

"I know we can," Dylan said. "Nick can skate a lot faster than he could last year."

"And Tommy, you've been working on your backhand shot a lot, right?" asked Nick.

"It's golden," said Tommy. "And don't forget about Dylan's slap shot."

"His slap shot was already great," Nick said.

"Yeah, but it's even faster now," said Dylan. "I can't wait to get on the ice and knock a few shots into the back of the net."

"There's nothing better than firing a slap shot past the goalie," said Tommy.

"Nothing better," Dylan agreed. He jumped up from the table. "Except for maybe landing a 720. Watch this."

Dylan raced across the skate park. He skated back to the top of the tall ramp. Tommy and Nick both skated after him.

"Have you ever tried a 720 before?" asked Tommy. He sounded a little nervous.

"I don't know, man," Nick said. "Maybe this isn't such a good idea."

"I'll be fine," Dylan said. "Piece of cake."

With that, Dylan pushed himself down the ramp. He flew across the ground, up the smaller ramp, and into the air. He turned his body. He needed to do two full revolutions before landing on his skates.

The first spin was perfect, but the second one was sloppy. Dylan couldn't keep his body tucked in tight enough to complete the rotation. He was falling too quickly. The spin was going to be short.

At the last second, Dylan tried to rotate his upper body to finish the spin. Instead, the move threw him totally off-balance.

He crashed to the ground, landing hard on his right arm. Dylan hollered in pain. Tommy and Nick quickly skated over.

"Are you okay?" Nick asked. He crouched down beside Dylan.

"My arm hurts," Dylan said.

"Can you lift it?" asked Tommy.

Dylan tried to raise his right arm into the air. Pain immediately shot from his wrist to his elbow. "No, I can't," he said.

"I think it's broken," Nick said.

"It can't be broken," Dylan insisted. "What about hockey season?"

"Let's get you to a hospital," said Nick. "We can worry about hockey later."

"I can't believe it," said Dylan, flopping onto his back. "I just can't believe it."

CHAPTER 2
ON THE MEND

Ten weeks later, Dylan pushed through the large glass doors that lead into the Iron Valley hockey arena. He looked down at his right arm. His cast had finally been removed. His arm looked pale and skinny compared to his left arm.

Dylan had missed the first few weeks of the hockey season. He was happy to be back.

It's been ten weeks, Dylan thought. *I just want to get back on the ice.*

As he walked toward the ice, Dylan straightened out his arm, twisting his wrist back and forth. He'd tried to practice using his hockey stick at home the day before. His arm still felt stiff.

"Dylan!" Nick shouted. Nick skated over as Dylan walked down the steps toward the ice. Their team, the Rangers, was in the middle of practice.

"The daredevil is back!" yelled Tommy. He skated toward the sidelines. A long plume of ice sprayed up as he stopped directly in front of Dylan.

"How are you feeling, buddy?" asked Nick.

"Fine," said Dylan. "My arm is still a little weak, though. I'll definitely need to build up strength."

"When can you skate again?" asked Tommy.

"I can skate now," Dylan said. "But my doctor said I shouldn't practice with the team for another week. My arm needs to get used to being out of the cast."

"Bummer," Nick said. "But I guess a week isn't too bad."

"It means I can't practice until the Midwinter Meltdown," Dylan told his friends.

"That's okay," Tommy said. "We're awesome right now. We're undefeated."

"I know," said Dylan. "I've watched all the games from the bleachers, remember?"

"It's not like he's been living in a cave," Nick said with a laugh.

"Hey guys! Bring it in!" Coach Erickson called from across the ice.

The entire team skated to the boards, where Coach Erickson was standing. Dylan walked over and let himself through the swinging half door to the bench.

"Let's welcome back our teammate," said Coach Erickson. The guys applauded. "I hear you still need to take it easy."

"Just another week," said Dylan.

"No problem," said Coach Erickson. "We can wait a week to have our slap-shot star back for the Meltdown Tournament."

"He'll be back, all right!" said Nick.

"And what about you, team?" Coach Erickson asked. "Are we going to beat the East Lake Scouts this year and bring home the trophy?"

48
19

"Yeah!" the team shouted.

"I can't hear you!" the coach yelled.

"YEAH!" the team shouted even louder.

"The trophy is ours!" Tommy yelled. "We're going to win that thing and bring it home to show our moms!"

Everyone looked at him. The team was silent.

"Good one, Tommy," said Dylan.

The players broke out in laughter.

"Good to have you back, Dylan," said Coach Erickson.

"Good to be back, Coach," Dylan replied.

CHAPTER 3
BACK ON THE ICE

A week later, Dylan, Nick, and Tommy walked into the arena where the Midwinter Meltdown was being held.

Thirty rows below them, a team was already out on the rink, practicing.

"That's East Lake," said Dylan.

The East Lake Scouts were skating in unison. When their coach blew his whistle, the players stopped, changed direction, and skated in the other direction.

"Their skating is perfect," said Nick.

"It's not that perfect," said Dylan. "We'll be able to handle them."

Privately, though, Dylan wasn't so sure. He still hadn't been able to practice with the Rangers. When he'd tried to practice at home, his arm had felt sore and stiff.

"Let's go, guys," said Coach Erickson, walking up behind them.

The Rangers headed to the locker room to suit up. When they got back to the rink, the Scouts were still there, finishing up the last of their drills.

"Is it my imagination or are they even bigger than last year?" Dylan muttered.

"What do they feed them in East Lake?" asked Tommy. "Steaks for breakfast, lunch, and dinner?"

"I just hope they don't eat us for dessert," Nick said.

The Scouts coach blew his whistle. The team skated toward the Rangers.

"Look at these runts," a Scouts forward said as he skated closer. "Are you guys sure you're in the right place? The preschool tournament is down the street."

"Is that Travis Caulfield?" Dylan whispered to Nick.

"That's him," said Nick. "He was the leading scorer in the state last season. And the big guy next to him is Peter Stevens. He's a defender. I heard he knocked three guys out of games so far this year."

"We're at the right tournament!" shouted Tommy. "And we're going to smoke you guys in the championship."

"The championship?" Travis repeated, laughing. "Did you hear that, Peter? They think they're going to the championship!"

"You guys don't stand a chance," said Peter. "Besides, even if you do make the championship, we'll skate circles around you. Just like we did last year."

"Not this time," said Dylan.

"It's a new year," said Nick.

"And a new tournament," said Dylan. "We're going to win it this year."

"Break it up, guys!" Coach Erickson interrupted. "Rangers, get on the ice!"

"See you at the championship," Travis said with a smirk.

"Oh, we'll be there," said Dylan. "And we'll beat you."

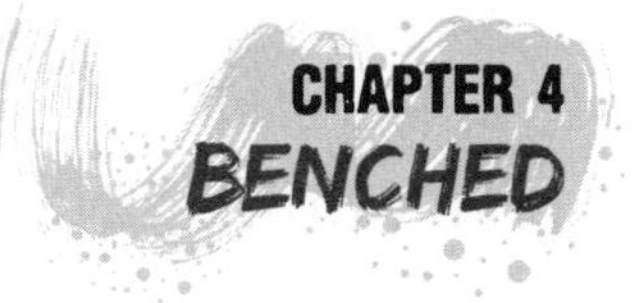

CHAPTER 4
BENCHED

Dylan skated backward across the ice. It felt smooth under the sharp blades of his skates. Nick and Tommy were beside him.

"Okay, guys," Coach Erickson shouted. "Let's do some warm-up drills."

"Feeling good, Dylan?" Nick asked.

"I feel great," said Dylan. "Like nothing ever happened."

"The three amigos are back!" said Nick.

"Enough talking, boys. Line up for the give-and-go drill!" shouted Coach Erickson.

The players took their places for the drill. Dylan and Nick lined up behind the goal, and Tommy skated out to the right circle. Another player lined up in the left circle, and two went out to the blue line. The Rangers goalie crouched in the net.

Coach Erickson blew his whistle. As Dylan watched, Nick passed the puck out to his teammate near the blue line. Nick skated hard toward the middle of the ice and received the pass back. Then he fired the puck quickly over to Tommy, in the circle, who immediately passed it back to Nick.

The puck hit the curve of Nick's stick as he skated toward the goal. He shot it hard past the goalie and into the net.

"Nice work, Nick!" Coach Erickson shouted. "Dylan, you're up."

Dylan's heart pumped. He couldn't wait to get the puck and blast it into the net. But he was nervous, too, and worried about his arm.

Coach Erickson blew the whistle.

Dylan quickly passed the puck to his teammate at the blue line. As he shot, a dull pain crept into his arm. He grimaced as he skated to the middle of the ice.

He passed the puck off to another teammate, and again, he felt an achy pain. "Ouch," he muttered.

Dylan pushed his skates hard off the ice and headed for the goal. He received the puck and flicked a hard wrist shot. Pain shot up his arm.

The goalie easily knocked Dylan's shot away from the net.

Shaking his head, Dylan took his spot back in the corner. *I have to get it together,* he thought. *We'll never beat the Scouts if I keep shooting like that.*

The team continued working on the give-and-go drill for several minutes. Each time Dylan tried the wrist shot, it was slow.

"Shoot it with power, Dylan!" shouted Coach Erickson from across the ice. "Let's see some speed!"

Dylan tried to shoot with the power he usually had. But his arm wouldn't cooperate.

Coach Erickson shook his head. Then he blew his whistle and called, "Slap shots! Line up for one-timers!"

Dylan skated across the blue line and over to the far boards. Coach Erickson stood on the blue line, near the center of the ice. He had a pile of pucks in front of him.

Coach Erickson flicked the puck across the ice. Dylan waited for it, raising his stick high into the air behind his body. As the puck cruised to him, Dylan pulled his stick down toward the ice.

Dylan's stick collided with the puck, sending it airborne toward the goal. It sailed smoothly into the back of the net. As his stick connected with the puck, Dylan felt the collision all the way up his arm. He closed his eyes briefly as pain shot from his wrist to his shoulder.

"Good one, Dylan," said Coach Erickson. He passed Dylan another puck.

Coach Erickson continued to pass him pucks, and Dylan fired shot after shot at the net. But each time he shot, the pain in his arm felt worse.

After several minutes of shooting, Coach Erickson held up his hand. "Nick!" he yelled. "Take over for me!"

Nick skated over and took Coach Erickson's spot in the center of the ice.

"Let's talk for a minute, Dylan," Coach Erickson said.

Dylan followed the coach over to the bench. Dylan took off his helmet and sat down next to his coach.

"I can tell your arm is still bothering you," Coach Erickson said.

"It's okay," said Dylan. "I'm fine."

"It's not okay if you can't play at full strength," said Coach Erickson. "Every player on the ice needs to give me a hundred percent."

"I can play," Dylan said. "I'll try harder. I'll keep practicing at home."

"I don't think so," Coach Erickson said, shaking his head. "I can't risk it. You could injure your arm more. And it wouldn't be fair to the team. I'm sorry. But I have to bench you for the tournament."

Coach Erickson stood and skated back to the center of the ice.

Dylan sighed in frustration and rubbed his arm. *Great,* he thought. *Now I won't help win the tournament.*

CHAPTER 5
WHAT'S THE POINT?

In the first game of the tournament, the Rangers took on the Apple Grove Muskies. Dylan didn't bother to suit up.

What's the point of wearing my uniform if I'm not going to be on the ice? he thought.

It killed him to be on the bench as his teammates spilled onto the ice.

"We're going to win this one for you, Dylan," Nick said.

"And the championship, too," Tommy added.

"Whatever," Dylan muttered.

Tommy and Nick both skated out and took their spots as forwards. Dylan watched from the bench as the referee dropped the puck at center ice, and the game began.

The action was slow as the teams tried to get the feel of the ice under their skates.

No one scored in the first two periods. With only five minutes left in the third period, Nick and Tommy teamed up. They flew down the ice, skating hard, with only one Muskies defender to stop them.

Nick passed Tommy the puck, and Tommy passed it right back. It was just like the give-and-go drill they had worked on during practice.

Nick received the puck and charged hard toward the right side of the net. With just ten feet between him and the goalie, Nick faked a pass to Tommy on the left. The goalie fell for the fake. He lunged to the left, leaving the entire right side of the goal wide open. Then Nick flicked an easy wrist shot into the back of the net.

The final two minutes of the game ticked away on the clock. The Muskies tried desperately to even the score, but they couldn't get past the Rangers' defense. As the buzzer sounded, Dylan glanced up at the scoreboard: 1-0, Rangers.

The Rangers celebrated their victory on the ice. Dylan stayed on the bench.

Game two was the next afternoon. Again, Dylan kept to himself on the bench.

The Rangers played even better than in the first game. They easily beat the Maple Park Orioles 3-1. The powerful scoring duo of Nick and Tommy was hard to beat. Nick scored two goals for the Rangers. Tommy scored the other.

After the game, everyone celebrated the victory in the locker room.

"We're going to the championship," Nick cheered.

"Just like we said we would," said Tommy.

"I wish I could be out there tomorrow," Dylan mumbled.

"You should talk to the coach," said Nick. "Maybe he'll change his mind and let you play."

"Yeah, we could really use you, man," Tommy agreed. "Even if you're not at full strength."

Dylan rubbed his arm. "Maybe you're right," he said.

Dylan walked over to where Coach Erickson was standing.

"What's up, Dylan?" the coach asked.

"I want to play tomorrow," said Dylan. "My arm feels a lot better. I want to be out there on the ice with my teammates. I want to help them beat the Scouts."

"That's not a good idea," Coach Erickson said with a sigh. "I know you want to play. But you've only had one practice with the team since your injury. I can't just put you into the finals with no practice."

"But I've been practicing at home," Dylan said. "And I've been to every single Rangers practice and game. Even if I haven't been skating, I've been paying attention."

Coach Erickson thought for a minute. "Is your arm really feeling better?" he asked.

"Yes," said Dylan. "I wouldn't play if it wasn't."

"I'll tell you what," said the coach. "Warm up with the team before the game tomorrow. If your arm is okay in warm-ups, we'll talk about you playing. But you have to tell me the truth. I don't want you to get hurt."

Dylan's smile covered his face. "You won't regret this!" he said. Then he raced over to his friends.

"What did he say?" asked Tommy.

"I'm in!" Dylan said.

"All right!" said Nick. "Now we'll beat those Scouts for sure!"

CHAPTER 7
TOO RISKY

The next afternoon, the Rangers warmed up on the ice. Dylan skated easily as he and his teammates glided in circles to warm up their legs.

Around the rink, other teams were warming up too. Dylan could see the Scouts skating nearby.

"Well, if it isn't the pipsqueaks from up north," said Travis Caulfield as he skated past.

Peter Stevens skated behind him. "Your opponents must have been a joke," he said. "I can't believe you guys made it to the championship game."

"Believe it!" Dylan said. "We made it here, and we earned it."

"Your team might have earned it," Travis said, "but you didn't. I heard you watched both games from the bench."

"That's enough, boys. Slap shots!" yelled Coach Erickson.

The Rangers quickly formed a line for the slap-shot drill. Dylan took a spot behind Nick. His arm didn't hurt, but he was still nervous. He didn't want to go first.

Nick took five passes from Coach Erickson and nailed five wicked slap shots into the net.

"Dylan, you're up!" the coach yelled.

Dylan skated into position. He looked at his arm. Then he closed his eyes for a second. "I can do this," he whispered.

The coach hit a slow wrist shot. Dylan raised his stick and swept it toward the puck. His stick and the puck met in a solid collision that he felt all the way up his arm. Dylan grimaced, but kept quiet.

Coach Erickson narrowed his eyes. "How's that arm?" he asked.

"It's okay, Coach," said Dylan. "Give me another one."

Coach Erickson frowned, but he fired another puck to Dylan.

Dylan wound up and shot the puck hard. This time, he couldn't help grabbing his arm in pain.

"That's enough," the coach said. "Your arm isn't better. Take a seat on the bench."

"No way," said Dylan. "I can do it."

"On the bench!" Coach Erickson yelled. "Not another word!"

Dylan threw his stick on the ice and skated toward the bench. He dropped down and put his head in his hands.

Nick skated to the bench with Dylan's stick in his hand. "Here you go," he said.

"I can't believe he benched me again," said Dylan, grabbing the stick.

"Your arm isn't ready," Nick said. "You know that."

"You're on Coach's side?" Dylan asked angrily. *I can't believe this,* he thought. *Even my best friend doesn't want me to play.*

"I'm not on anyone's side," Nick said. "I just think the coach has a good reason for keeping you out of the game."

"Oh, yeah?" muttered Dylan. "Why?"

"He doesn't want you to hurt your arm," said Nick. "And . . ." He looked away.

"And what?" asked Dylan.

Nick looked at Dylan. "The team might be stronger if you're on the bench," he said.

"Really?" asked Dylan. "So that's how it's going to be? You think the team will do better if I'm not playing?"

"I didn't mean it like that," said Nick. "But if you can't pass well and shoot hard, someone else can do a better job."

"Thanks a lot," said Dylan. "I thought we were friends."

"We are," Nick said. "And I thought you were a team player."

"Just leave me alone," Dylan snapped. "If you guys don't need me, maybe I should just go home."

"We need you, Dylan," said Nick. "We need your eyes from the bench. You can still help us win."

"Whatever," Dylan said. *Obviously Nick doesn't think I'm good enough,* he thought angrily.

Nick stared at him for a moment. Then he shook his head and skated back onto the ice.

Dylan slumped back on the bench. He watched as the teams prepared for the game. *I shouldn't have even put on my jersey,* he thought. *What a waste.*

CHAPTER 8
MIDWINTER MELTDOWN

In the first period, the Scouts were like a machine. They skated easily around the rink and scored an early goal. The Rangers tried to keep up, but the Scouts were bigger and faster.

Dylan didn't cheer for his teammates at all. He was too angry. He was angry at Coach Erickson for benching him, and he was angry at his friends for not supporting him.

Most of all, Dylan was angry with himself. He knew Nick was right. The team was better off with him on the bench. But he was upset to be missing the championship game.

After the first period, the Scouts led 1-0. Between periods, Coach Erickson talked to the team in the locker room.

"Guys, we're not skating as hard as we can," he said. "And our passing isn't as sharp as it should be. Lead your teammates down the ice. I want to see more shots. We can't score if we don't shoot. Am I right?"

"Right, Coach!" the team yelled together.

Coach Erickson looked at Dylan. "How about you, Dylan?" he asked. "Is there anything you've noticed that could help us win?"

"Nope," Dylan said. He shook his head. He knew he was being a bad sport. But he couldn't be enthusiastic when he was being forced to watch the game from the bench.

"Okay, guys," Coach Erickson said. "Let's tie this thing up!"

The players cheered. Then they started walking back to the rink.

Nick and Tommy cornered Dylan in the hallway. "We need to talk," Nick said.

"You're being a jerk," said Tommy.

"What are you talking about?" Dylan asked.

"I know you're upset you can't play," said Nick. "But you're part of this team."

"We need your help if we're going to win this game," said Tommy.

"You'll see so much from the sidelines that we miss," Nick added.

Dylan was quiet for a minute. *Tommy and Nick are right,* he thought. *I am being selfish. Just because I can't play doesn't mean I'm not a Ranger.*

"Well, there is one thing," Dylan said. "I noticed that Travis likes to skate to his right. If you cut him off and force him to his left, you'll throw him off balance."

"See! I told you you'd see stuff we didn't!" Tommy shouted.

"Thanks, Dylan," said Nick. "Keep the tips coming, okay?"

Dylan smiled. "Okay," he said.

Together, the three friends turned and marched back to the rink.

CHAPTER 9
A PART OF THE TEAM

As the second period started, Dylan was on his feet.

"Let's go, guys!" shouted Dylan. "Force the action! Crisp passes!"

The Rangers were much quicker on their skates in the second period. They were keeping up with the Scouts, and limiting their scoring chances. Nick was forcing Travis to his left every chance he got, just like Dylan had told him.

Five minutes into the period, one of the Scouts was called for tripping and sent to the penalty box for two minutes. That gave the Rangers a power play. They would have an extra player on the ice for two minutes. It was the perfect chance to tie the game.

Right away, the Rangers tried to score. Nick fired two different shots on goal. Tommy shot one at the net. But the goalie for the Scouts blocked all three shots.

"Keep shooting, guys!" Dylan called to his teammates. "One of them will go in!"

But after the two-minute power play, the Rangers were still scoreless.

The instant the penalty was over, the Scouts player flew out of the penalty box. Travis and Peter charged down the ice with him. Tommy and Nick were back to defend.

Travis had the puck on his stick. Peter danced around Tommy to the left, while Travis smoothly sailed past Nick to the right.

"Put a body on him!" shouted Dylan. "Don't go for the puck. Go for the body!"

Travis flicked an easy pass to Peter, who made the perfect shot past the Rangers goalie and into the net. The score was now 2-0.

"We need to put a body on them," Dylan repeated to himself.

With the Scouts ahead by two goals, the Rangers increased their intensity on defense. Peter lived up to his reputation as a hard hitter. He seemed to knock every Rangers player onto the ice. The Rangers had a hard time getting any shots on goal.

GUEST
2
7:32
HOME
0
PERIOD 2
PENALTY 1
PENALTY 2
48
SHAW
48
REEVES
63
63

Near the end of the period, Nick made a rush toward the net. He looked back toward Tommy, who was controlling the puck. Nick received the pass, then turned toward the goal. Instantly, he was met by a crushing blow from Peter. He hit the ice hard.

Dylan looked up at the scoreboard. The clock counted down. 3-2-1. The horn sounded, signaling the end of the second period.

In the locker room, Coach Erickson tried to keep his team upbeat. "We still have one period to go, guys," he said. "We just need two goals to tie."

"Can I say something, Coach?" Dylan asked.

"Um, sure, Dylan," said Coach Erickson. "Go ahead."

Dylan cleared his throat. "Here's how I see it, guys," he said. "The Scouts are skating around us because we aren't checking them at the blue line. We need to play the man, not the puck. We need to make some good, hard checks out there and knock them off their game. They like to skate. They don't like to hit."

"Peter likes to hit," said Tommy.

"Yeah, he does," said Dylan. "But so do you, right, Tommy?"

"Right," said Tommy.

"Then you handle Peter," said Dylan. "Stay on him this entire period."

"But the guy is built like a truck," Tommy said.

"You can do it, Tommy," Dylan said. "We all have faith in you. Right, team?"

"Right," the rest of the team echoed.

"And the rest of you," said Dylan. "Get physical and knock them off their game, okay?"

"Okay!" the team shouted.

The players stood and headed back toward the rink. Nick hurried to Dylan's side.

"Thanks, Dylan," Nick said.

"No, thank you," said Dylan. "Thanks for reminding me that I'm still part of the team. It doesn't matter if I'm on the ice or on the bench."

"Let's go win this thing," Nick said.

"Let's do it!" Dylan yelled.

At the start of the third period, Travis and Peter passed the puck back and forth across the blue line. Nick and Tommy were back playing defense for the Rangers.

Travis flicked the puck over to Peter. Tommy had a chance to knock the puck away, but instead, he drove his body into Peter's chest. He slammed into him and knocked him off the puck.

"That's the way to do it!" shouted Dylan.

Nick swiped the puck with his stick and quickly passed it forward. Tommy skated hard down the left side of the ice, and Nick skated down the middle.

The Rangers player passed the puck back to Nick, who sent it across the ice to Tommy. Nick darted around a defender and skated toward the goal. Tommy flicked the puck back to him.

Nick received the pass, faked the goalie to his right, and swept across the goal for a backhand. The puck hit the back of the net.

"Goal!" shouted Dylan. He shared a fist bump with Coach Erickson.

The Rangers continued to take Dylan's advice. They were putting their bodies on the Scouts, and Tommy was shadowing Peter nonstop.

The strategy was working. The Scouts didn't get a shot on goal for the first six minutes of the third period.

The Scouts were getting frustrated. As Tommy took the puck down the ice, Peter swung his stick hard at Tommy's knees. The referee blew his whistle. Peter was called for slashing and sent to the penalty box.

"Nice," Dylan whispered.

The Rangers took advantage of the second power play. Nick skated behind the net as Tommy positioned himself in front of the goal. Nick faked out a player rushing toward him and passed the puck to Tommy. Tommy did a one-timer, meeting Nick's pass with an immediate slap shot.

The goalie never had a chance. The puck sailed past him into the net.

"Goal!" shouted Dylan. "It's all tied up!"

There were only two minutes left in the game. "No overtime, guys!" Dylan shouted. "Let's win this thing right now!"

The clock continued to count down as Nick, Tommy, and the other Rangers tried to control the puck. But on a bad pass from Tommy, Travis intercepted the puck. Only Nick was nearby to stop him from scoring.

"Force him left," Dylan yelled.

Nick skated backward, staying in front of Travis. But Travis tried to skate around Nick and go right.

"Play the body!" shouted Dylan.

Nick waited for the right opportunity, and then lunged forward. He put his shoulder and elbow into Travis's chest, forcing him to the left and off the puck.

Travis lost his balance and stumbled. The puck was left wide open.

"Go, Nick!" Dylan shouted.

Nick reached for the puck and pushed it forward. He crossed the blue line. Tommy skated toward the right side of the goal. Nick fired a pass in his direction.

Tommy took two hard strides around his defender and blasted a wrist shot high above the goalie's shoulder. The shot was perfect. It sailed into the net.

"Goal!" shouted Dylan. He turned to Coach Erickson for a high-five.

Ten seconds were left on the clock. The Rangers were ahead, 3-2.

Dylan counted down as seconds ticked away. The final horn sounded. Everyone, including Dylan, stormed the ice.

"That was a team victory all the way!" Coach Erickson shouted. "Here you go, guys!" He handed the Midwinter Meltdown trophy to Nick and Tommy.

Nick and Tommy lifted the trophy high above their heads. "Dylan, get in here!" shouted Nick.

"You guys won it," Dylan said, shaking his head. "You deserve to carry it."

"We all deserve to carry it," said Tommy. "This is a team win, and you're part of the team."

Dylan lifted the trophy high above his head, and the team cheered. "We're the champs!" Nick shouted.

"And next year I'll actually get to be on the ice," Dylan said. "The Scouts won't know what hit them!"

ABOUT THE AUTHOR

Thomas Kingsley Troupe writes, makes movies, and works as a firefighter/EMT. He's written many books for kids, including *Legend of the Vampire* and *Mountain Bike Hero,* and has two boys of his own. He likes zombies, bacon, orange Popsicles, and reading stories to his kids. Thomas currently lives in Woodbury, Minnesota with his super cool family.

ABOUT THE ILLUSTRATOR

When Sean Tiffany was growing up, he lived on a small island off the coast of Maine. Every day until he graduated from high school, he had to take a boat to get to school! Sean has a pet cactus named Jim.

GLOSSARY

championship (CHAM-pee-uhn-ship)—a contest or final game of a series that determines which team or player will be the overall winner

collision (kuh-LIZH-uhn)—a forceful crash, often at high speed

dominate (DOM-uh-nate)—to control or to rule

enthusiastic (en-thoo-zee-ASS-tik)—excited or interested in something

injury (IN-juh-ree)—damage or harm

tournament (TUR-nuh-muhnt)—a series of contests in which a number of people or teams try to win the championship

regret (ri-GRET)—to be sad or sorry about something

revolution (rev-uh-LOO-shuhn)—a rotation or spin

DISCUSSION QUESTIONS

1. Why do you think Coach Erickson decided to bench Dylan, even though Dylan said his arm was okay? Do you think he made the right decision?

2. What do you think about Dylan's attitude when he got benched? Was he right to be upset, or was he being a bad sport?

3. Which hockey postion is the most difficult to play? Talk about your choice. What do you think makes it so difficult?

WRITING PROMPTS

1. Tommy and Nick helped Dylan realize that he could still help the team, even if he couldn't play. Write about a time a friend helped you see something from a new perspective.

2. Has an injury ever stopped you from doing something you love? Write about what happened.

3. Who do you think was the most valuable player on the Rangers team during the championship game? Dylan, Tommy, or Nick? Why?

HOCKEY POSITIONS

A hockey teams is made up of six players: five skaters plus one goalie on the ice at a time. While each player has a specific job to do throughout the course of the game, they must also work together to form a solid team. Here's a rundown on the different positions:

GOALIE — The goalie is responsible for keeping the puck out of the net. Many think this is the most difficult position on a hockey team. Some famous goalies are Patrick Roy, Glenn Hall, Dominick Hašek, and Kyle Dryden.

DEFENSEMEN — There are two defensemen in a hockey game, one for the left side and one for the right side. The main goal of this position is to stop the opposing team from taking shots on the goal. Some of hockey's most famous defensemen are Chris Chelios, Scott Stevens, Nicklas Lindstrom, and Bobby Orr.

WINGS — There are two wings in a game, the right and left wing. These players are the other two forwards on the ice. They focus on the outside of the ice, near the side boards. Wings are typically physical players who are good along the boards and in the corners. Some famous wings are Brett Hull, Guy Lafleur, and Gordie Howe, who is often called "Mr. Hockey" and thought to be one of the greatest hockey players of all time.

CENTER — The center is one of three forwards on the ice, making this an offensive position. This player focuses on the center of the ice, away from the side boards. The center must be a strong skater and able to do face-offs. A center is a creative player who focuses on passing to the wingmen. Some of the most famous centers of all time are Steve Yzerman, Mario Lemieux, Eric Lindros, and Wayne Gretzky, who is often called "The Great One."